The Diary

of

Robin's Toys

Ken and Angie Lake

Donkey

Hoo-Tee

Published by Sweet Cherry Publishing Limited
53 St. Stephens Road,
Leicester, LE2 1GH
United Kingdom

First Published in the UK in 2013

ISBN: 978-1-78226-027-1
Text: © Ken and Angie Lake 2013
Illustrations: (c) Vishnu Madhav,
Creative Books

Title: Donkey Hoo-Tee - The Diaries of Robin's Toys

Printed and Bound By Nutech Print Services, India

Every Toy Has a Story to Tell

Have you ever seen an old toy, perhaps in a cupboard, or in the attic or loft? Have you ever seen how sad they look at car boot sales, unwanted and unloved? Well, look at them closely, because every toy has a story to tell, and the older, the more decrepit, the more scruffy, the more tatty the toy is, the more interesting its story could be. Here are just a few of those toys and their stories.

It was Sunday morning, and Robin pulled back the curtains and looked out at a steamy street. The weather was what Mum called *muggy*. It was going to be a hot day at the car boot sale.

Robin raised his eyes from his drawing for a moment and looked towards the house across the road. Francesca, his new friend, was standing at the window and she gave him a friendly wave.

Robin smiled and waved back.

It had been about a week since the Hetfields moved in to the house.

There were three children: Francesca and Marcella, who were twin sisters and about Robin's age, and a little baby brother called James.

Even though Francesca and Marcella were twins, they were not identical and their personalities were very different.

Francesca was outgoing, always outside playing and made friends easily; Marcella was the exact opposite, and was really shy.

She spent most of her time in her room painting and couldn't really relate to anyone.

She had to wear a hearing aid and often had problems keeping up with conversations because the other children forgot that she had trouble hearing them.

Francesca explained to Robin that her sister didn't like playing with other children because she felt that everyone always had to make a special effort to include her.

She liked to stay indoors and paint. She tried to lose herself in her hobby, as if nothing else mattered.

Her mum knew that she was not happy, and really wished Marcella had someone she could relate to.

Robin's thoughts were interrupted by a familiar beep, beep ... beep, beep!

Grandad's little red car had arrived; it was time to go to the car boot sale.

"Good morning, Grandad."

"Good morning, Robin. Did you have a good week at school?"

"Yes, I did. Mr Hammet gave me an A in art!"

"An A? That's wonderful, Robin! Although I'm not at all surprised; you are a very talented artist. This Mr Hammet sounds like a good teacher."

"Oh yes, he is, Grandad. He takes a great interest in our work and spends a lot of time with each of us helping us to improve our drawing. You can tell that he really loves his job.

"Not all of the teachers are like Mr Hammet. I don't think all teachers love their work."

"That's probably very true, Robin; sad, but true."

Grandad had trouble finding a parking space when they arrived at the car boot sale; it was very, very busy.

He gave Robin 50 pence with his usual advice.

"Here you go, Robin,
50 pence. Spend it wisely."

They started making their way round the stalls.

Unfortunately, there seemed to be a lot of second-hand clothes, which both Robin and Grandad found really boring.

They walked around and around looking for toys, but there really wasn't much on offer ... or perhaps all the best toys had been sold.

"Oh look, Robin, that looks like a fun stall: Fanny's Fancy Dress."

"Okay, let's have a look."

There were all sorts of treasures: princess outfits, superhero costumes, caveman costumes ... just about every fancy dress outfit you could imagine.

There was a very nice hat
with feathers on it, and
Grandad remembered that
Grandma had been looking for
one just like it to wear for her
amateur dramatics production
of *Chitty Chitty Bang Bang.*

"That hat is just what your grandma is looking for. When we come back this way later, I'll pick it up for her," said Grandad. "But now let's go and find you that special toy."

Eventually, they spotted Jason's Jumble.

"Good morning, Jason," said Grandad.

"Oh, good morning, lads. Nice to see you both again! What can I do for you today?"

"We were wondering if you have any interesting toys this morning?" said Robin.

"I don't know if I have any left. It's been a very busy morning and most of them have been sold. Let's have a look..."

Jason started digging around in a box under the table and emerged with a rather tatty-looking donkey.

"I'm afraid that this little fellow is the last toy. I don't think anyone wanted him because he's a bit old."

"Oh, we don't mind about that," said Robin. "What do you think, Grandad?"

Grandad had a good look
at the donkey. Then he went
into a little trance and
whispered a few words to him...
He looked down at Robin and
nodded.

"Yes, Robin, this is a very interesting donkey indeed," he said.

"How much do you want for him, Mr Jumble?" Robin asked.

"Oh, shall we say 50 pence?"

"Perfect! Here you are."

"Thank you, young man. Shall I put him in a bag for you?"

Then Grandad and Robin returned to Fanny's Fancy Dress stall to pick up the hat for Grandma.

"Morning," said Grandad. "I'd like to buy that posh hat with the feathers you had on your stall earlier."

"I'm very sorry," said Fanny, "but I'm afraid I have just sold it. But I do have some other hats."

"Well, I can't go home empty-handed. Let's see if there's something else that we can make do with."

They had a good look through all the boxes: fireman helmets, top hats, traffic warden caps...

"I can't see anything, Grandad," said Robin.

"There must be something," replied Grandad.

"Here, what about this one?" said Fanny, producing a pirate's hat from a box in the boot of her car.

"Well, I'm not sure," said Grandad. "The other one had some feathers on it."

"Oh, that's not a problem," said Fanny. "I have the rest of the costume here. We'll just pluck some feathers off this stuffed parrot and no one will ever know the difference."

"Perfect!" said Grandad.

And with that, it was time to get back to the car and go to Grandad's house for their tea.

Hmmm ... something smells nice! thought Robin as he opened the front door.

"Good morning, Robin. I've made you boys some of my special lemon curd tarts." said Grandma.

"Good morning, dear," said Grandad as he walked into the kitchen. "I picked this up for your play."

Grandad handed the bag to Grandma, and she seemed slightly puzzled as she looked inside.

"Are you sure this is what they wear in *Chitty Chitty Bang Bang*?"

"Oh yes, absolutely, dear, without a shadow of a doubt."

Grandad winked at Robin.

"There was a costume stall at the car boot sale, and the lady there assured me that this hat was worn in the original film, by the leading lady."

"Oh, how wonderful, Harry! Now I'll be sure to get the leading role. Right, you boys have your tea. I'm going to rehearse my lines."

Grandma made a theatrical exit, leaving Grandad and Robin to eat their lemon curd tarts.

They sat down and removed Donkey from the bag, and put him on the kitchen table.

Then Grandad cast his magic spell.

"*Little toy, hear this rhyme,*
Let it take you back in time,
Tales of sadness or of glory,
Little toy, reveal your story."

Donkey twitched his little nose, opened one eye and pricked up his ears. Then he yawned that couldn't-care-less donkey yawn, rubbed his eyes and looked around.

"Hello, who are you?"

"My name is Robin, and this is my grandad."

"Very pleased to meet you. My name is Hoo-Tee, Donkey Hoo-Tee."

"Hoo-Tee?" said Robin. "What sort of name is that for a donkey, or anything else for that matter?"

"Well, Robin, let's just say that it's a sort of Spanish name."

"How did you come to get a name like Hoo-Tee?"

"*If you must know, my mother gave it to me. She had heard the name somewhere and she thought it came from a character in a Spanish book, but she wasn't really sure. Anyway, that's the name that she gave me, and that's the name I have always answered to.*"

"Oh, I see. Hoo-Tee, will you please tell us something about yourself?"

"Yes, okay. Are you both sitting comfortably?"

"Yes, we are."

"Good, then I shall begin.

"I am a proper Spanish donkey; I was born there and grew up there. Now, if your geography is a bit duff,

Spain is in southern Europe (that's the bottom bit of Europe). Spain joins with France at the top and with Portugal to the left.

"I lived in a little village on the plains of La Mancha, somewhere near the middle of Spain.

"La Mancha is big, usually hot and dry, and is well known for its wine, sunflowers and old windmills.

"But now for the really interesting bit, my story. It was early one Spanish autumn morning. There was dew on the ground and the sound of crickets filled the air. Cheep, cheep! That's the sound that crickets make.

"Someone had told me that crickets make that noise by rubbing their legs together. I had tried to do it several times, but I just got sore knees.

"I was a working donkey, just like all of my friends. We were known as pack animals, because our owners would pack lots of things onto our backs and make us carry them.

"So that was my job, but I didn't enjoy it. Well, would you? I had my own straw baskets which were strapped to me, and these would be loaded with whatever needed to be carried.

"My owner was a peasant; that's not an insult, almost everybody was a peasant. This man's name was Pedro, but all the donkeys called him Fandango, because he danced up and down and shouted when he got angry.

"It was an insult for the donkeys to call him Fandango, but he didn't speak donkey, so he never knew.

"Anyway, on this particular morning I was loaded with my straw baskets as usual. It was autumn and the olive-picking season was in full swing. We trotted out of the village and along the terraces until we came to Fandango's olive grove.

"There were already several people there, because they all helped each other at olive-picking time.

"Nets were spread out
on the ground, and some
people whacked the olive trees
with sticks so that the olives
dropped into them.

"Other people were picking
out the leaves and twigs, and
then more people were loading
the olives into my baskets.

"I looked around and
yawned; it was one of those
couldn't-care-less donkey
yawns.

"I had seen all of this before and I can tell you that I didn't like it much.

"Life was difficult for me and for my master; food was scarce and there was very little money. The work was hard, the sun was hot and the days were long.

"I dreamed of lazing around all day, eating proper hay and drinking fresh clean water.

"I really wanted my own farm. I always had the same dream, but would it ever come true?

"The load of olives was very heavy and I trudged through the terracing to where they would be dried in the baking sun. They would be turned for several days to concentrate the oil, and then I would have to carry them back into the village to be pressed.

"The olive oil was very important, as it was stored and used for cooking, and any that was left over could be sold."

" Donkey Hoo-Tee, what happened next?"

"Do be patient, Robin, I am just getting to the interesting bit.

"So that just about summed up my life: carry, carry, stop, then carry again. That is why I was known as a beast of burden, but that description didn't please me much either.

"If I wasn't carrying olives, I was carrying melons, or grapes, or grain. And to add insult to injury, if there was nothing to carry, Fandango would park his fat bum on my back. It was all getting too much to bear!

"Anyway, it was another of those long mornings, and I was plodding out through the terraces when something caught my eye.

"It was something I had seen before, and I thought it might be valuable. I made a mental note of where it was, and then got on with my work.

"It was about 2 o'clock in the afternoon and the sun was scorching. Fandango had finished his bread and cheese and half a bottle of red wine, and was lying down, fast asleep.

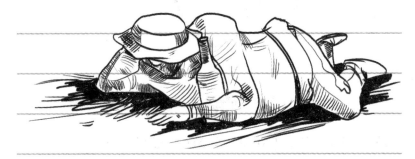

"This is what the Spanish call a Siesta.

"His snoring could be heard for miles. Now's my chance,

I thought. So I trotted back to where I had seen the valuable object, and it was still there.

"I grabbed it with my teeth and hid it under my basket straps. I was excited for the first time in years.

"That evening, I showed my treasure to my clever donkey friend, Dario.

" 'Do you know what you have there?' he said.

" 'Err no, not really, Dario.'

" 'Well, Hoo-Tee, you have found some money; that's a one hundred Peseta note!'

" 'Oh, is it really? And what can I buy with it?'

" 'You can get some wine and lots of those smelly cigarettes'.

" 'That's no good to me', I said, 'I don't smoke and I don't drink wine.'

" 'Well,' said Dario, 'if I were you, I would buy a ticket for the state lottery. You could win a fortune.'

"So that's what I did."

"When Saturday night came round, I gathered with some of my donkey friends outside the bar in the village. There was a crackly old radio inside, and at 8 o'clock every Saturday some boys would sing out the winning lottery numbers.

"Lots of the peasants were sitting inside the smoky bar, clutching their tickets and hoping - and even praying - for their numbers to come up.

"As the last number was read out, the bar fell silent. Then there was moaning and groaning, and ripping of tickets. There were loud sighs and echoes of, 'Oh well, better luck next week.'

"But I wasn't feeling sad at all, and my face had quite a different expression; every one of my numbers had come up! I asked my clever friend Dario to double-check my ticket. He was almost speechless.

" 'Hoo-Tee, you have won enough money to buy your own farm! You will never have to work again!'

"I was, as you say, over the moon when I heard that.

" 'Okay, Dario, where do I get my money from?' I asked.

" 'Err, well, really sorry about this, Hoo-Tee, but you can't actually claim the money because you are a donkey, and donkeys aren't allowed to play the lottery.'

"I could not believe it. For the first time in my life I had played the lottery and had a winning ticket, but was excluded from getting my money because I was a donkey!

"My dreams of retirement were shattered; I would have to work hard forever!

"I mooched around for several days, not speaking to anyone, but I kept the ticket to remind me of what might have

been. Then, one morning, Dario
and I had to carry some olive oil
to the market in the next
village.

   "As we entered the village,
I saw a nice-looking house
behind a big hedge.

   "So, just to make
conversation, I said to Dario,
'Who owns that big house?'

" 'Oh, that nice house,' Dario replied, 'belongs to the man you were named after. He is quite famous for helping people and for his honesty.

'That is the house of DON QUIJOTE (Don Key Hoo-Tee) of La Mancha. You have exactly the same name, except that your mother spelt it wrong.'

" 'Who did you say?' I asked, wanting Dario to repeat the name.

" 'Look, you do realise that in Spain a Don is a very well-respected and important type of man?'

" 'Yes, Dario, I know that.'

" 'Well, that house belongs to a famous Don: DON QUIJOTE, (Don Key Hoo-Tee),' replied Dario.

" 'Wow, he must be very important if my mother named me after him.'

" 'Oh yes, he is famous all over Spain. He used to be quite an adventurer.'

"I forgot all about my work and ran straight up to the big house, determined to meet the famous man that my mother had named me after.

"I rang the doorbell and waited for the well-known man

of action to appear ... but he was taking his time.

"I could hear some rattling noises, so as the gate was open I walked into the yard.

" 'Don Quijote, Don Quijote!'
I shouted as I looked around
for him.

"To my surprise, I wasn't
greeted by a young adventurer,
but by a rather tired-looking
old man who was ploughing a
little plot of land.

" 'Don Quijote! I shouted,
'What is a famous adventurer
like you doing ploughing a field?'

" 'I'm not an adventurer any more,' he answered. 'I'm just a lonely old man that nobody visits.'

" 'Don't worry,' I said, 'I am an old donkey, but I'm sure that if I help you, we can plough that field in no time.'

"And that's what we did, we ploughed the field together, and we talked and talked.

"By the evening, Pedro discovered that I had escaped and he followed my trail to Don Quijote's farm.

"He came chasing up the driveway, saying, 'There you are, you stupid animal!'

"He apologised to Don Quijote for me escaping and bothering him, and raised a stick to whip my hind legs, but Don Quijote stopped him.

" 'Wait!' he said. 'Don't hit the donkey. He's old and has had a hard life.'

" 'He's old and useless,' said Pedro.

" 'In that case, let me buy him,' said Don Quijote.

"I was stunned! Pedro set a price, not a very high one ... and Don Quijote agreed.

" 'Thank you, Mr Quijote,'
I said when Pedro had gone. 'It
will be a true honour to work
for you.'

" 'Oh, I don't want you to
work for me,' Don Quijote
replied. 'I think that after all
our hard work we can grow old
together and help each other.'

"I was so touched! This was better than having my own farm.

"Finally, I had someone who understood what I was going through because he was going through the same thing too, and I didn't feel so alone!

"So it was an extra-special surprise for Don Quijote when I gave him the winning lottery ticket.

"At last I had a best friend to share my winnings with, and do you know what we did with the money? We opened a donkey retirement farm, so that donkeys that were too old to work could have somewhere nice to rest.

"Of course, you know who's really to thank for all these wonderful things that happened to me? I'll tell you. It's thanks to my mum, for giving me such a silly name!"

"Wow, Donkey Hoo-Tee, you really have had an interesting life," said Robin.

"Is that the time?" said Grandad. "I had better get you home, young man."

Later the following week, Robin received a phone call from Grandad.

"Hello, Robin? I just wanted to know how Donkey Hoo-Tee is settling in with you."

"Oh, he's fine, Grandad; but how is Grandma?"

"She's very busy at the moment. You remember that hat we bought her at the car boot sale? Well, it's landed her the leading role in the play."

"Oh really, Grandad? In *Chitty Chitty Bang Bang*?"

"No, in *Pirates of the Caribbean.*

"She wants us to go back to the car boot sale this weekend and pick up an eyepatch and a wooden leg! Anyway, how is your week going?"

"Very well, Grandad, but I'll have to tell you all about it on Sunday. I have to go across the road to see some friends."

"Alright, Robin, see you!"

"Bye, Grandad."

Robin had some very important business to attend to. You see, on Sunday when he got home from Grandad's house, he had gone to see his new neighbours.

He had asked to borrow some of Marcella's artwork.

On Monday morning, he had taken Marcella's paintings to his art teacher, Mr Hammet.

Mr Hammet was so impressed that he had called Mrs Hetfield, Marcella's mum, to offer to give Marcella art lessons.

When Robin went to return Marcella's paintings, Mr Hammet was already there, talking to Marcella about paints and shading and colours. And Robin knew this was the beginning of a very nice friendship.